Luna Loves ART

Joseph Coelho

Fiona Lumbers

Kane Miller
A DIVISION OF EDC PUBLISHING

Luna Loves Art.

Today she is going on a school trip.

School trip backpack – check!
School trip lunch box – check!
School trip instant camera – click!

Dad drops Luna off at the school gates.
Miss Rosa is waiting to take attendance.
Luna's mom is a chaperone!

Finn is alone.

Today the class is going to The Art Gallery.

The whole class is excited.
The gallery is the biggest building
Luna has ever seen.

But Finn doesn't care. Finn is looking down.

They start off in a huge room
full of amazing massive things,
full of color,
full of shapes.

"Look at all the art!" says Luna.
Finn is looking up.

Miss Rosa takes the class to The Impressionist and Post-Impressionist Rooms.

Vincent van Gogh's *Sunflowers* has paint so thick that the flowers look alive.

Finn goes to touch it.
"Stop!" says Luna. "You're not allowed to touch the paintings!"

Miss Rosa hands out some clipboards, paper and pencils. Luna does a sketch ... Scribble!

Finn scrunches up Luna's picture! "Hey!" says Luna.

Miss Rosa takes
Finn aside.

"Why is he so mean?"
says Luna.
"Maybe he needs a
friend," says Mom.

Miss Rosa takes the class to The Abstract Paintings Room.

Kazimir Malevich's *Black Square*
is all edged, black and cracked.
A nighttime robbed of stars,
a phone waiting to ring.

Finn's mouth is open.
"Do you want to sketch
with me, Finn?" asks Luna.

Finn is silent.

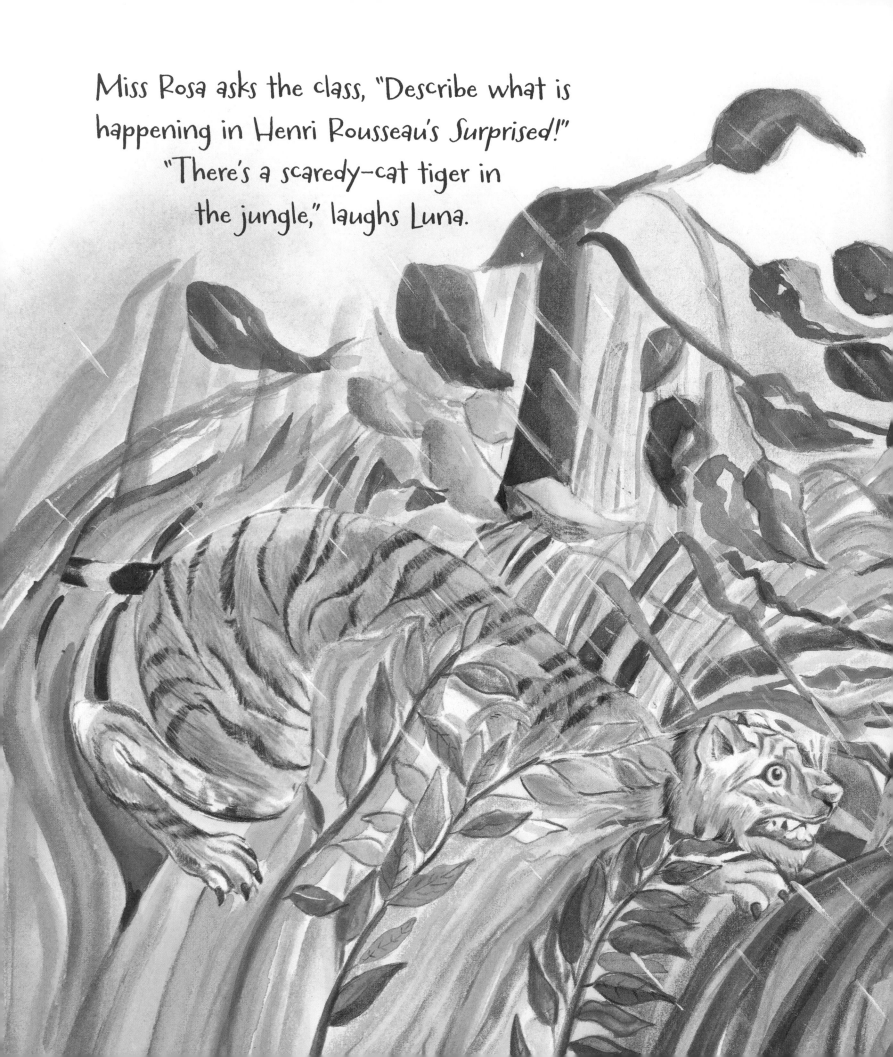

Miss Rosa asks the class, "Describe what is happening in Henri Rousseau's *Surprised!*" "There's a scaredy-cat tiger in the jungle," laughs Luna.

Finn roars at the painting ...
"The wind is thrashing, the clouds are dark.
The tiger is angry,
but inside he is cold and wet.
He wanders the jungle
staying in different places all the time.
The tiger is scared and alone
and needs a home."

Mom leads Finn to a quiet corner.
Luna follows.
Henry Moore's *Family Group*
is big and bronze.
Luna takes a photo ... Click!
"Families don't look like that," says Finn.

Mom says ...
"Some families look like that, some do not.
Some families are related, some are not.
Some families are together, some are apart,
there are lots of different families like all this different art."

Miss Rosa takes the class to a dark room,
full of lights and sounds.
"We can touch the art!" beams Luna.
"It's incredible," shouts Finn.

Everyone looks different
under the pulsing lights.
One big colorful family.
Luna takes a photo ... Click!

Miss Rosa takes the class to The Art Gallery Shop.
There are erasers, pencils and buttons.
Henry Moore key rings, posters of sunflowers and
black squares, postcards of tigers.
Toys that light up and flash.

Luna gives Finn a photo.
Finn gives Luna a drawing.

Luna and Finn laugh
on the bus back to school,
take photos of the sights
and talk about the art they remember.

Luna and Finn love school trips.
Luna and Finn love art.

Jackson Pollock

Piet Mondrian *Composition II in Red, Blue, and Yellow, 1930*

Édouard Manet
Girl with summer hat,
Jeanne Demarsy, 1879

Paul Cézanne
Still Life, Pears
and Green Apples,
1873

Pierre Bonnard
*Woman at a
Table, 1923*

Andy Warhol
Flowers, 1964

Henri Matisse
*Blue Nude II,
1952*

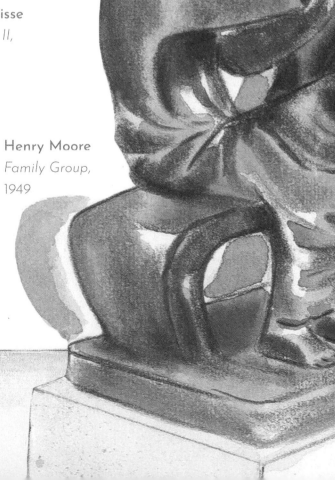

Andy Warhol
*Campbell's
Soup Can, 1962*

Henry Moore
*Family Group,
1949*

Acknowledgments

Damien Hirst, *Untitled 2* (Spot Painting), 1992 © Damien Hirst and Science Ltd. All rights reserved, DACS 2019.

Andy Warhol, *Flowers*, 1964 © 2019 The Andy Warhol Foundation for the Visual Arts, Inc./Licensed by DACS, London.

Andy Warhol, *Campbell's Soup Can*, 1962 © 2019 The Andy Warhol Foundation for the Visual Arts, Inc./Licensed by DACS, London.

Louise Bourgeois, *Maman*, late 1990s © The Easton Foundation/VAGA at ARS, NY and DACS, London 2019.

Louise Bourgeois, *Untitled* (Suspended Sculpture), 2004 © The Easton Foundation/VAGA at ARS, NY and DACS, London 2019.

Henri Matisse, *Blue Nude II*, 1952 © Succession H. Matisse/DACS 2019.

Henri Matisse, *The Snail*, 1953 © Succession H. Matisse/DACS 2019.

Henry Moore, *Family Group*, 1949 © The Henry Moore Foundation. All Rights Reserved, DACS/www.henry-moore.org.
Reproduced by permission of The Henry Moore Foundation.

Jackson Pollock © The Pollock-Krasner Foundation ARS, NY and DACS, London 2019.

Yayoi Kusama, *Pumpkin* (Red), *Pumpkin* (Yellow), 2016 © Yayoi Kusama.

Jeff Koons, *Balloon Dog*, 1994-2000. Used with permission from the artist.

For all you little artists out there who have found joy in art, be it in the looking at, immersion in or creation of this wonderful expression that is for us all. – J.C.

For Sonny & Teddy.
And special thanks to Beccy & Sue. – F.L.

First American Edition 2020
Kane Miller, A Division of EDC Publishing

First published in Great Britain in 2020 by Andersen Press Ltd.,
20 Vauxhall Bridge Road, London SW1V 2SA
Text copyright © Joseph Coelho 2020
Illustration copyright © Fiona Lumbers 2020
The moral rights of the author and illustrator have been asserted.

For information contact:
Kane Miller, A Division of EDC Publishing
P.O. Box 470663
Tulsa, OK 74147-0663
www.kanemiller.com
www.usbornebooksandmore.com

Library of Congress Control Number: 2019952226

Printed and bound in China
1 2 3 4 5 6 7 8 9 10
ISBN: 978-1-68464-046-1